101 Brain Booster

Activity Book

Wonder House

Jumbo Trail

Help the little elephant find his mum.

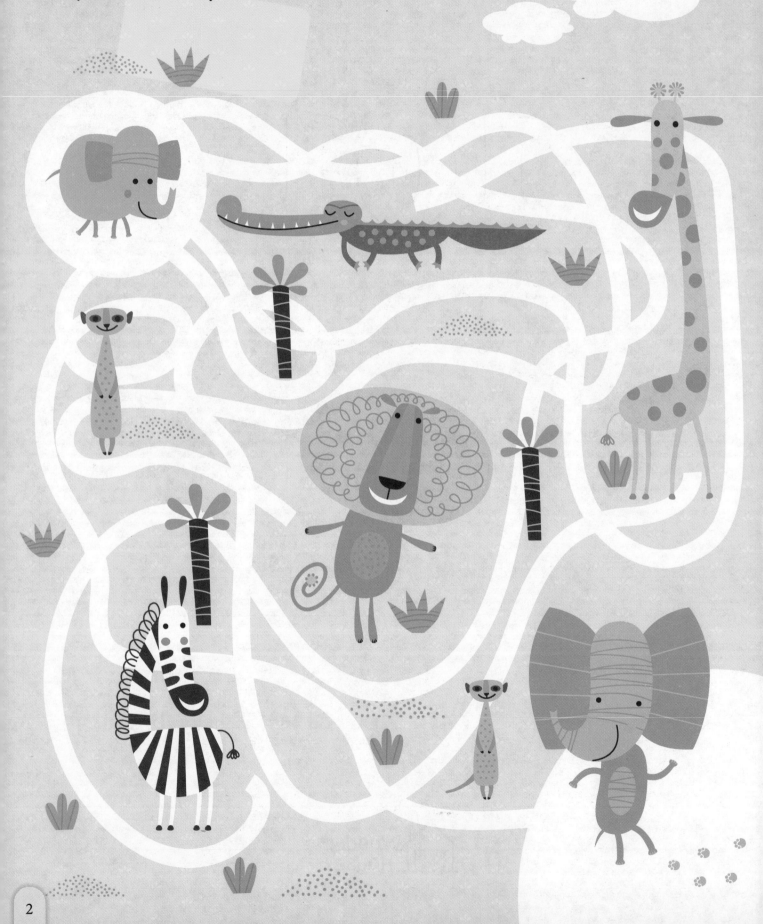

Shadow Match

Match the animals of the cat
family with their shadows.

A

B

C

D

E

1

2

3

4

5

Dino Sculpt

Connect the dots and color the picture brightly.

11
12
13
14
15
16
10
17
9
18
8
7
6
5
19
3
4
20
2
1
21
22
23
24
26
25
27
30
29
28

Home Search

Help the creatures reach their home.
The first one is done for you.

Pasture Fun

Can you spot 10 differences in the two pictures given below?

Pumpkin Patch

Find the exact mirror copy for each row and match the pairs.

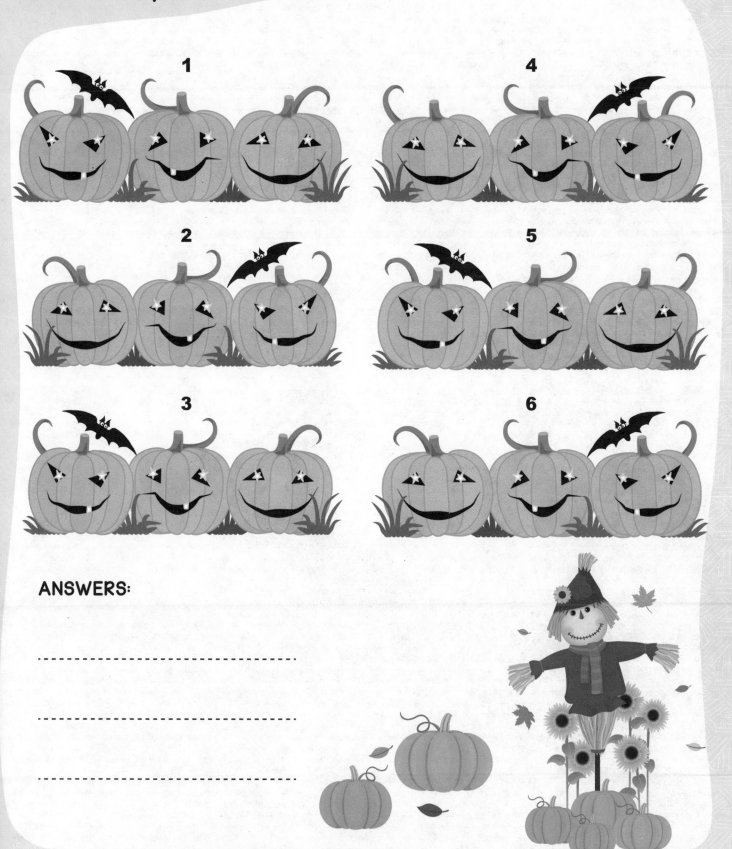

1

4

2

5

3

6

ANSWERS:

Broom Flight

Find the correct shadow of the witch on the broom.

Picture Perfect

Find and circle two identical pictures.

A

B

C

D

1

2

3

4

Animal Pairs

Find and match identical animals.
The first one is done for you.

Animal Crossword

Solve the animal crossword using the picture clues.

Bear Sculpt

Connect the dots and color the picture brightly.

Cheese Trail

Help the hungry mouse reach
the yummy cheese.

Happy Squirrels

Can you spot 5 differences between the two pictures below?

Freddy's Barn

Help Freddy count the animals in his barn.

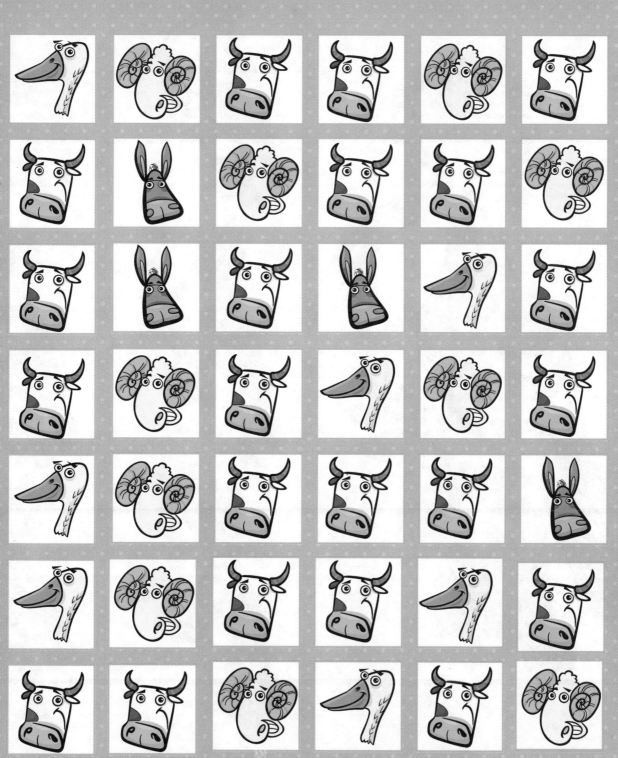

Shadow Match

Find the correct shadow of the woodpecker.

Sand Castle

Help the panda climb the correct set of ladders to reach his friends at the top.

Hopping Trail

Fill the missing numbers and help the frog reach the stone.

Frog Sculpt

Connect the dots and color the picture brightly.

Evening Stroll

Spot 10 differences between the two pictures.

Zoo Animals

Complete the picture by identifying the missing patches. Draw the correct shape in the space given below.

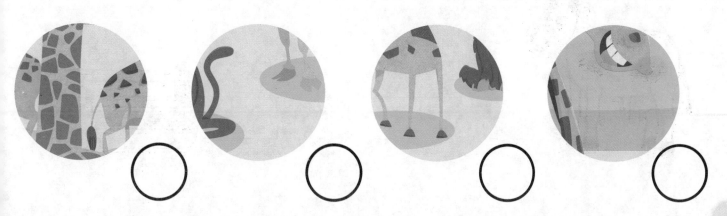

Horizontal Patterns

Trace the patterns and help the animals reach their homes.

Things That Move

Match the vehicles with their mode of transportation.

Healthy Veggies

Solve the crossword with the help of picture clues.

Yummy Treat

Choose the yummy food which will complete the sequence.

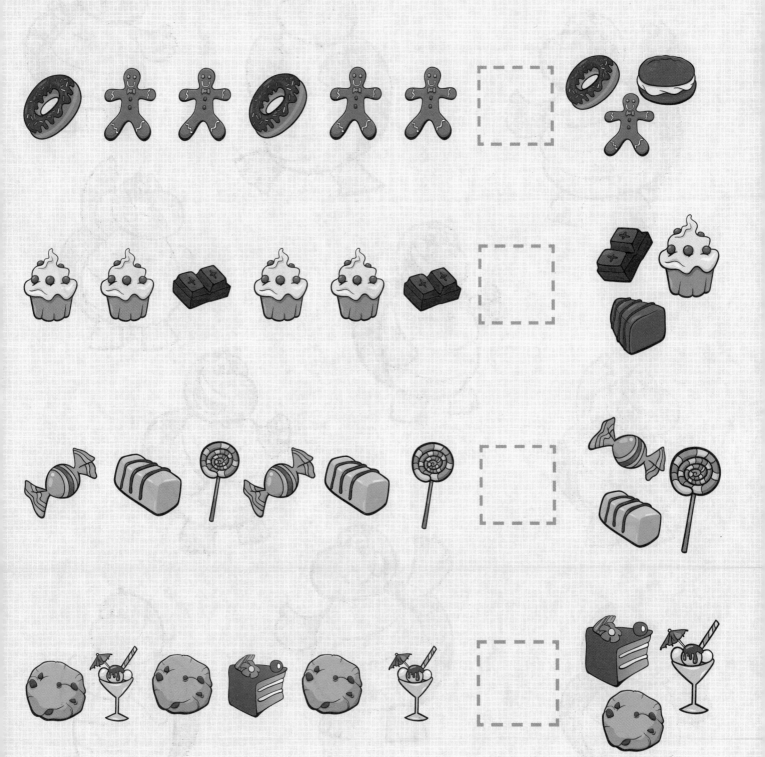

Turtle Twins

Find and match the turtle twins in the picture.
The first one is done for you.

Entangled Giraffes

Free the entangled giraffes by connecting the numbers on the neck with the correct letters on the head.

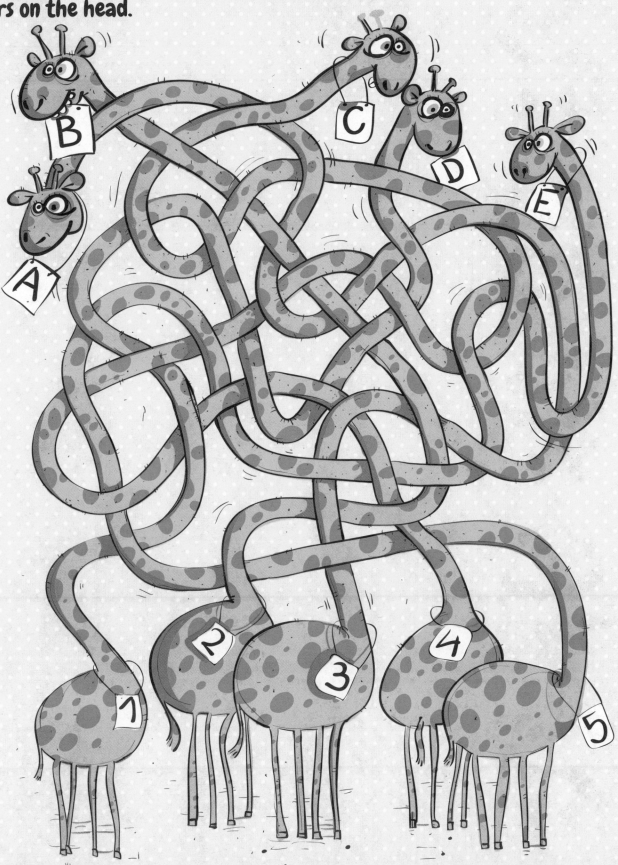

Exercising Panda

Match the pandas with their shadows.

A

 1

B

 2

C

 3

D

 4

E

 5

Identical Twin

Find the identical image of the monkey on the left.

Grazing Cows

Find 5 differences between the two pictures below.

Honey Quest

Help the baby bear find his favorite food while avoiding the bees.

HONEY

Expressive Dogs

Find and circle two identical pictures.

Colorful Decorations

Count the objects and write the
answers below.

Answers

Dancing Monkeys

Match the monkeys with their correct shadows.

Safari Fun

Spot 10 differences between the two pictures given below.

Jingle All The Way

Find two identical Santas in the picture and circle them.

Jumbo Sculpt

Connect the dots and color the picture brightly.

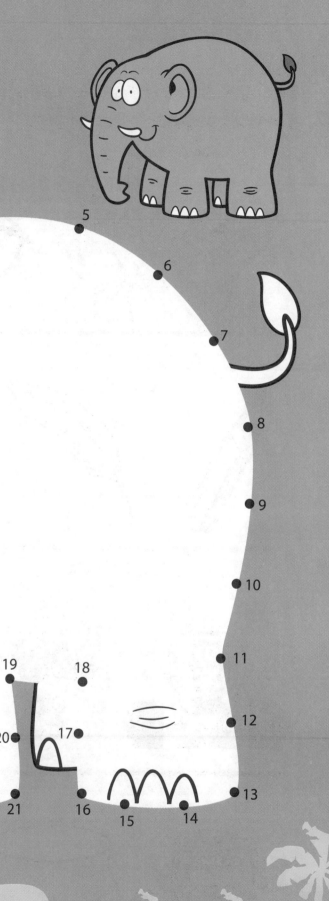

Odd One Out

Find and circle the picture which does not belong to the group.

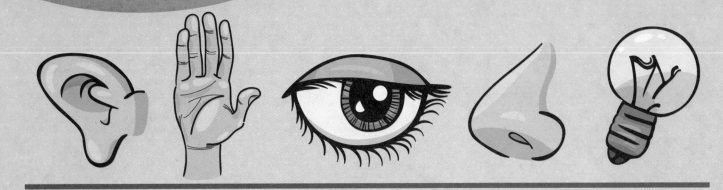

Shadow Fun

Find and circle the correct shadow of the children playing around the tree.

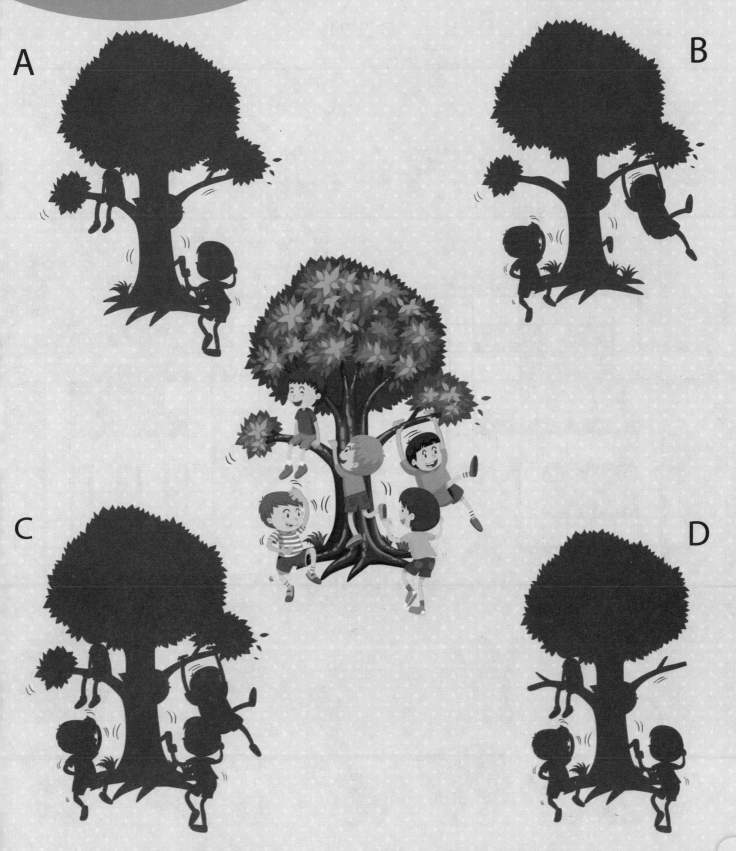

A

B

C

D

Zoo Visit

Use the picture clues to solve the crossword puzzle.

DOWN

ACROSS

Jungle Animals

Match the animals with their shadows.

Monkey Sculpt

Connect the dots and color the picture brightly.

Pirate Ship

Find 10 differences between the
two pictures drawn below.

Animals in the Farm

Use the picture clues to solve this crossword puzzle.

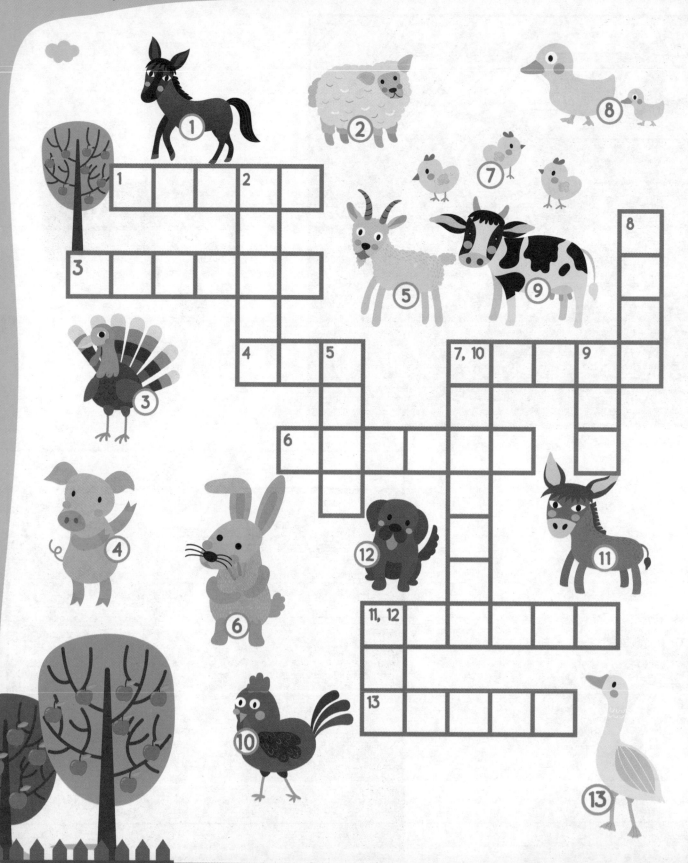

Farm Graze

Complete the picture by identifying the missing patches. Draw the correct shape in the space given below.

1 ◯   2 ◯   3 ◯   4 ◯

Space Travel

Spot 10 differences between the two pictures drawn below.

Lion Sculpt

Connect the dots and color the picture brightly.

Animal Queue

Complete the sequence by choosing
the correct animal.

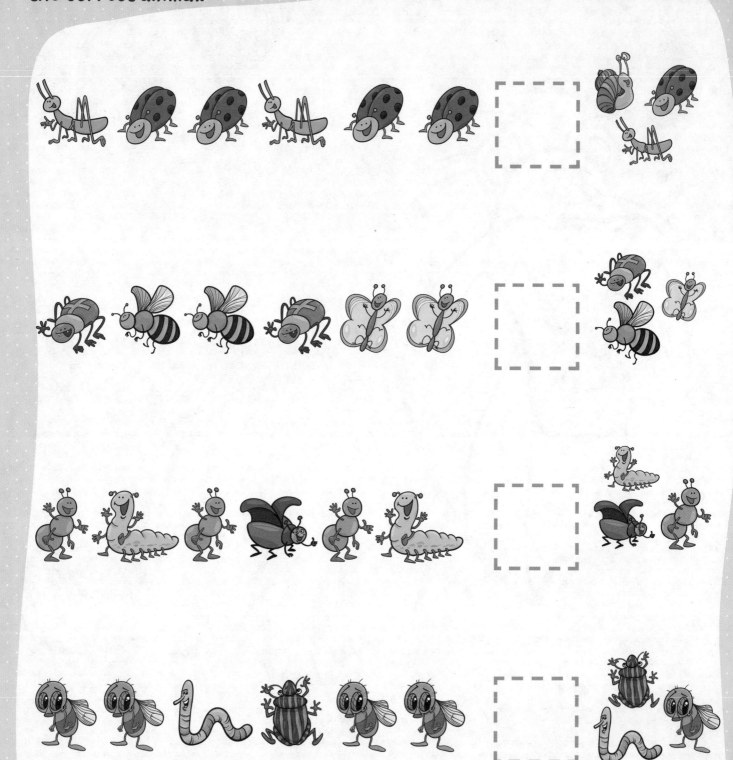

Nut Quest

Help the squirrel grab the nut by finding the correct path.

Soccer Fun

Find the correct shadow of the soccer player.

Easter Egg

Help the painter find the right path to the giant Easter egg.

Mismatched Pictures

Can you match the faces of these cute animals with their bodies?

The Misfit

Find and circle the odd one out.

Toucan Sculpt

Connect the dots and color the picture brightly.

Animal Cruise

Find 10 differences between the two pictures drawn below.

Polar Trail

Help the baby polar bear find its mother.

Under The Ocean

Use the picture clues to solve the marine animals' word search puzzle.

F	S	Q	U	I	D	B	E	A	G	E	N
O	T	H	A	F	O	W	H	A	L	E	K
E	S	R	T	R	E	I	N	D	O	E	R
H	E	R	M	I	T	C	R	A	B	A	K
N	A	R	D	H	A	S	H	F	S	L	D
S	H	A	R	K	E	T	U	R	T	L	E
E	O	F	L	A	R	B	Z	A	E	P	B
O	R	I	R	M	A	N	T	A	R	A	Y
P	S	K	U	I	M	I	V	S	E	R	S
H	E	I	S	O	C	T	O	P	U	S	O
P	I	T	L	E	R	N	H	A	L	O	T
D	O	L	P	H	I	N	I	C	R	A	B

Squid   Whale   Lobster   Turtle   Shark
Sea Horse   Hermit Crab   Octopus   Manta Ray   Dolphin

57

Snail Trail

Help the snail find its way to its yummy food.

Spot The Odd One

Find and circle the odd one out in each row.

Hot Desert

Solve the desert animal crossword using the picture clues.

African Safari

Solve the African animals' word
search puzzle using the picture clues.

C H E C K G I R A F F E
H O L U N D U W E G U I
I Z E B R A E I C O Y W
Q P P T H C K U D U I I
O J H F I Z E D T I N L
S B A R N T S P O W E D
T L N S O E O B H A R E
R O T S C E Y Z U N K B
I E D R E A L E L U O E
C O W L R U I S V B I E
H I P P O P O T A M U S
T U R K S Y N A T H I T

Giraffe   Zebra   Wildebeest   Hare   Lion
Elephant   Ostrich   Hippopotamus   Rhinoceros   Kudu

Owl Sculpt

Connect the dots and color the picture brightly.

Bat Terror

Spot 10 differences between the two pictures drawn below.

Skating Snowmen

Match each snowman with its correct shadow.

Jigsaw Puzzle

Identify the correct piece of the jigsaw puzzle to complete the picture of the lion.

1   2   3

Sportsmen

Help these players find their right sports equipment.

Missing Pieces

Match the letters with the right numbers
to complete the picture.

1   2   3   4   5

Polar Animals

Solve the polar animals' word search puzzle using the picture clues.

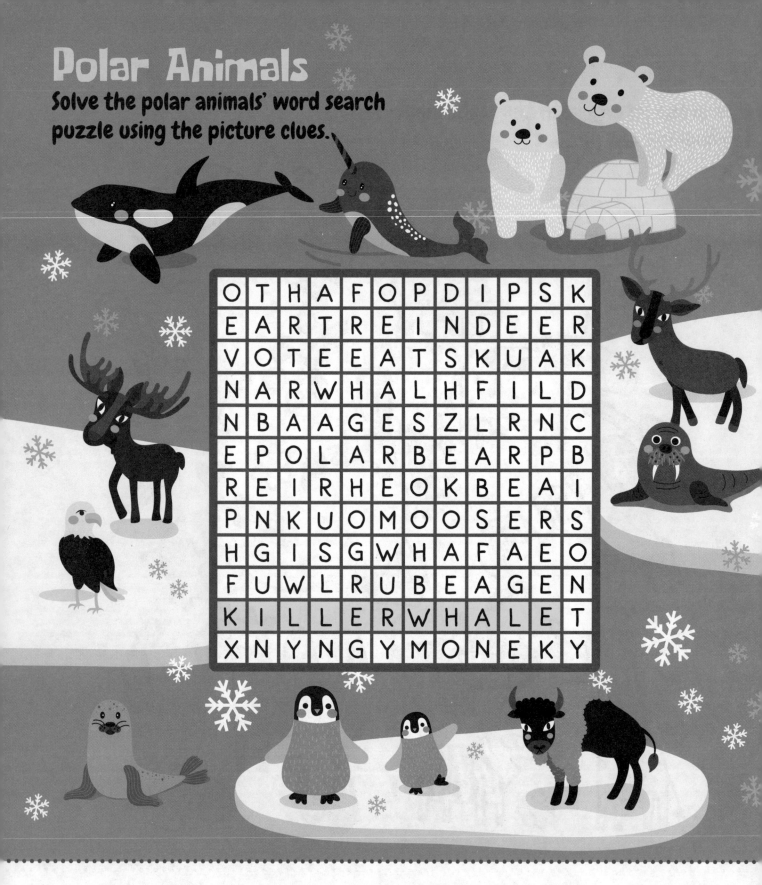

O	T	H	A	F	O	P	D	I	P	S	K
E	A	R	T	R	E	I	N	D	E	E	R
V	O	T	E	E	A	T	S	K	U	A	K
N	A	R	W	H	A	L	H	F	I	L	D
N	B	A	A	G	E	S	Z	L	R	N	C
E	P	O	L	A	R	B	E	A	R	P	B
R	E	I	R	H	E	O	K	B	E	A	I
P	N	K	U	O	M	O	O	S	E	R	S
H	G	I	S	G	W	H	A	F	A	E	O
F	U	W	L	R	U	B	E	A	G	E	N
K	I	L	L	E	R	W	H	A	L	E	T
X	N	Y	N	G	Y	M	O	N	E	K	Y

Polar Bear   Penguin   Killer Whale   Moose   Eagle

Walrus   Reindeer   Narwhal   Seal   Bison

Panda Sculpt

Connect the dots and color the picture brightly.

Parking Area

Help the driver park the car in
the parking area.

Missing Animals

Match the letters with the correct shapes to complete the picture.

A

B

C

D

E

F

G

Horse Pair

Find the exact mirror image of each horse and match the pairs.

Jungle Dance Party

Match the dancing animals with their shadows.

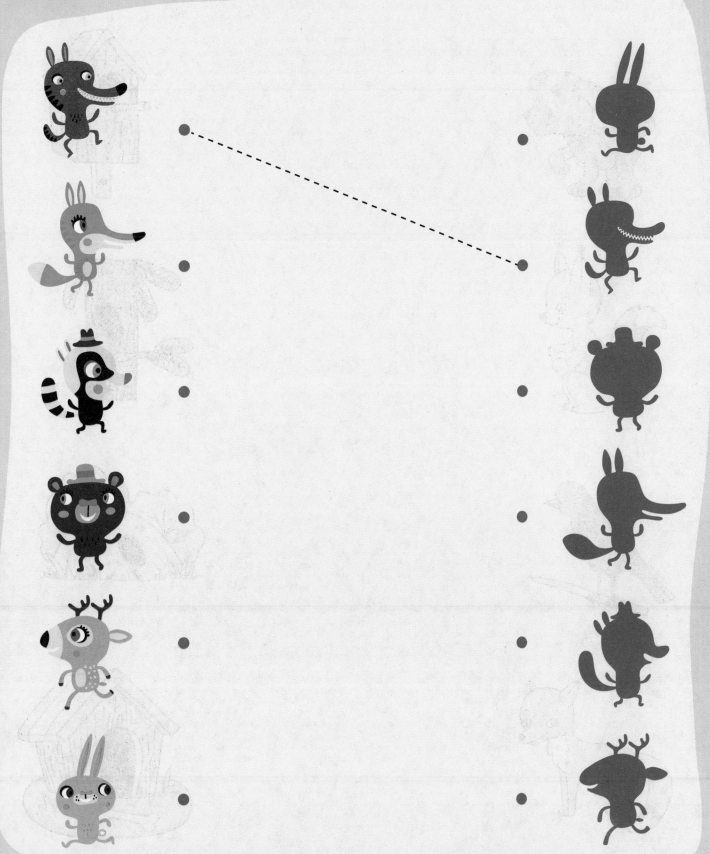

Cozy Homes

Help the animals reach their homes
before nightfall.

At The Farm

Solve this farm animals' word search puzzle using the picture clues.

C	H	I	C	K	A	Z	S	H	O	R	E
H	O	S	U	N	D	U	F	E	G	U	N
I	L	M	V	B	U	E	X	C	O	W	E
Q	P	R	T	I	C	K	S	U	A	I	Y
K	J	D	O	N	K	E	Y	T	T	N	C
D	B	O	R	A	T	S	N	O	W	E	H
R	L	G	O	N	E	O	K	N	A	M	I
A	O	N	S	H	E	E	P	U	N	R	C
B	E	D	R	O	O	M	I	L	U	N	K
B	O	W	L	R	U	N	G	O	O	S	E
I	N	D	O	S	K	Y	B	I	S	M	N
T	U	R	K	E	Y	W	I	T	H	I	N

Duck **Donkey** **Chicken** **Goose** **Sheep** **Dog**

Chick **Horse** **Turkey** **Rabbit** **Pig** **Goat**

Bird Count

Count the birds and write the answers below.

76

Puppy Sculpt

Connect the dots and color the
picture brightly.

Underground Trail

Help Buzzy cross the underground maze and reach its yummy food.

In The Swamp

Find 10 differences between the two pictures drawn below.

Jumping Reindeer

Match the reindeer with their correct shadows.

Elephant Jigsaw Puzzle

Identify the correct piece of the jigsaw
puzzle to complete the picture.

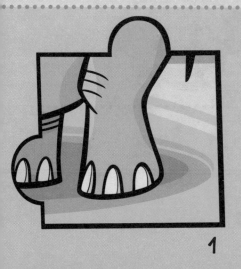

1

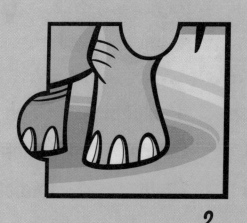

2

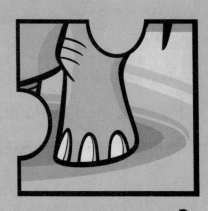

3

Healthy Vegetables

Solve the vegetable word search puzzle using picture clues.

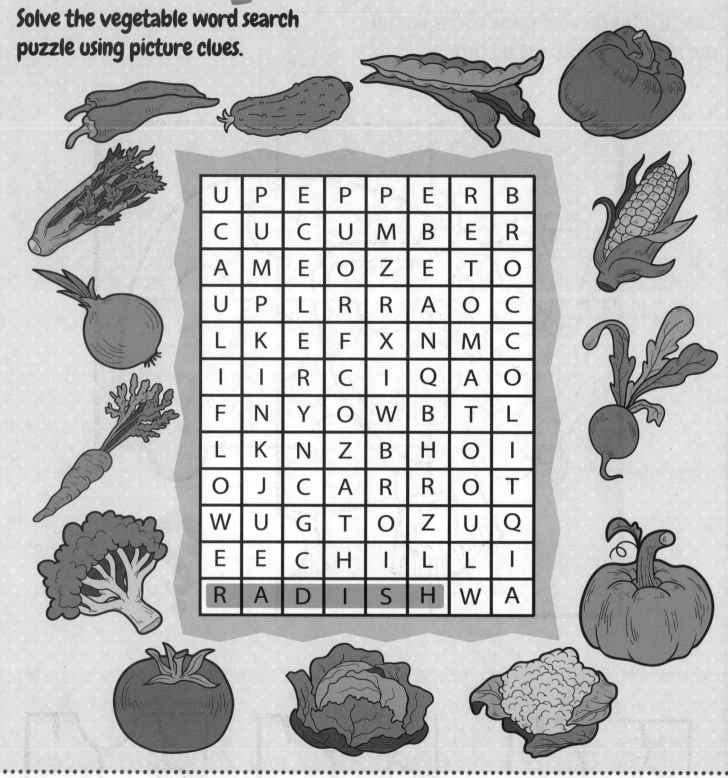

U	P	E	P	P	E	R	B
C	U	C	U	M	B	E	R
A	M	E	O	Z	E	T	O
U	P	L	R	R	A	O	C
L	K	E	F	X	N	M	C
I	I	R	C	I	Q	A	O
F	N	Y	O	W	B	T	L
L	K	N	Z	B	H	O	I
O	J	C	A	R	R	O	T
W	U	G	T	O	Z	U	Q
E	E	C	H	I	L	L	I
R	A	D	I	S	H	W	A

Pepper   Cucumber   Pumpkin   Corn   Bean

Tomato   Broccoli   Carrot   Onion   Cauliflower

Celery   Cabbage   Chilli   Radish

Missing Frames

Find the fragments which will complete the picture.

Night Stroll

Spot 10 differences between the two drawings.

Cloud Trail

Help the dinosaur reach its hungry babies.

Sports Mismatch

Can you find the 6 mistakes that the artist made while drawing the picture?

Pool Fun

Find the correct shadow of
the boy.

Garden Fun

Count the animals and write the number in the space given below.

Out Of Place

Find and circle the odd one out.

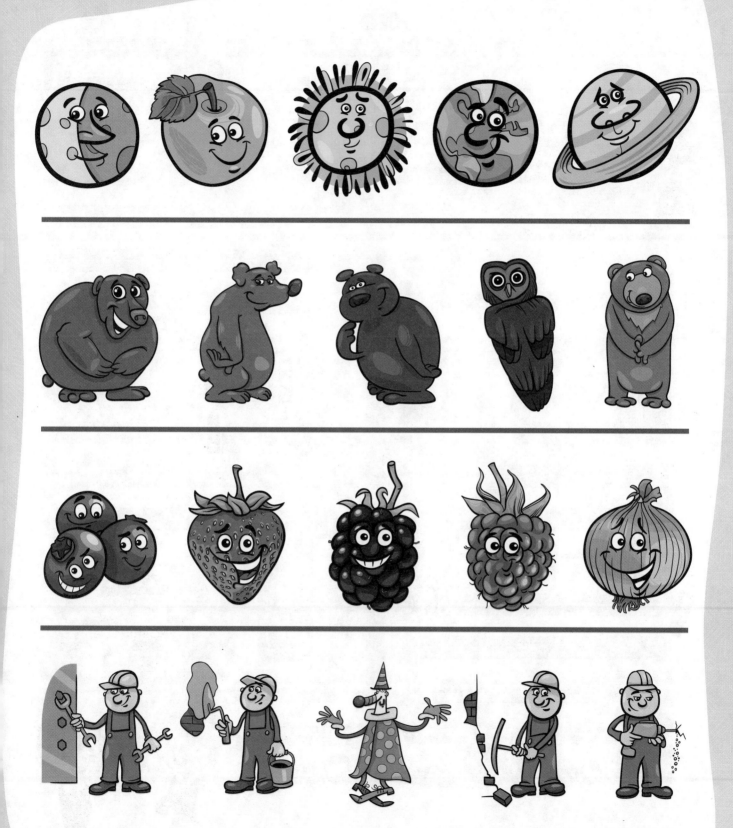

City Travel

Help the kids reach school on time.

Koala Sculpt

Connect the dots and color the picture brightly.

91

Fruit Salad

Solve the fruit word search puzzle using the picture clues.

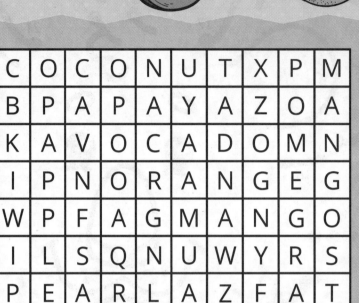

C	O	C	O	N	U	T	X	P	M
B	P	A	P	A	Y	A	Z	O	A
K	A	V	O	C	A	D	O	M	N
I	P	N	O	R	A	N	G	E	G
W	P	F	A	G	M	A	N	G	O
I	L	S	Q	N	U	W	Y	R	S
P	E	A	R	L	A	Z	F	A	T
P	E	R	S	I	M	M	O	N	E
W	D	Q	Z	G	U	A	V	A	E
O	Z	A	P	R	I	C	O	T	N
P	I	N	E	A	P	P	L	E	R

Coconut   Banana   Kiwi   Guava   Mango

Papaya   Mangosteen   Pomegranate   Orange   Apricot

Persimmon   Pineapple   Pear   Avocado   Apple

Animal Homes

Help the animals reach their houses.

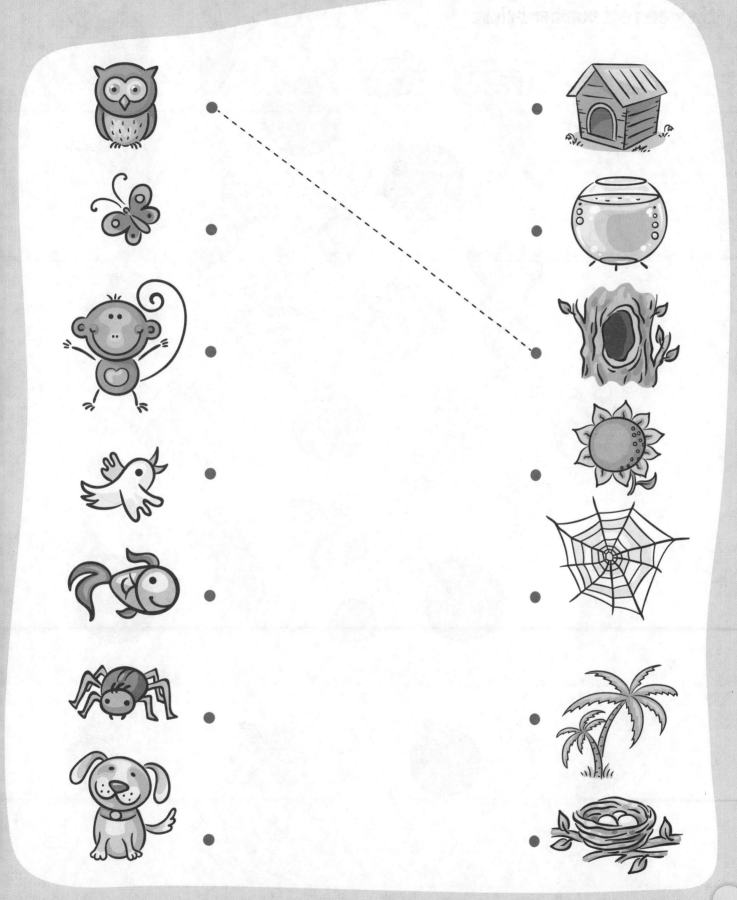

Farm Produce

Count the fruits and vegetables and write their correct number below.

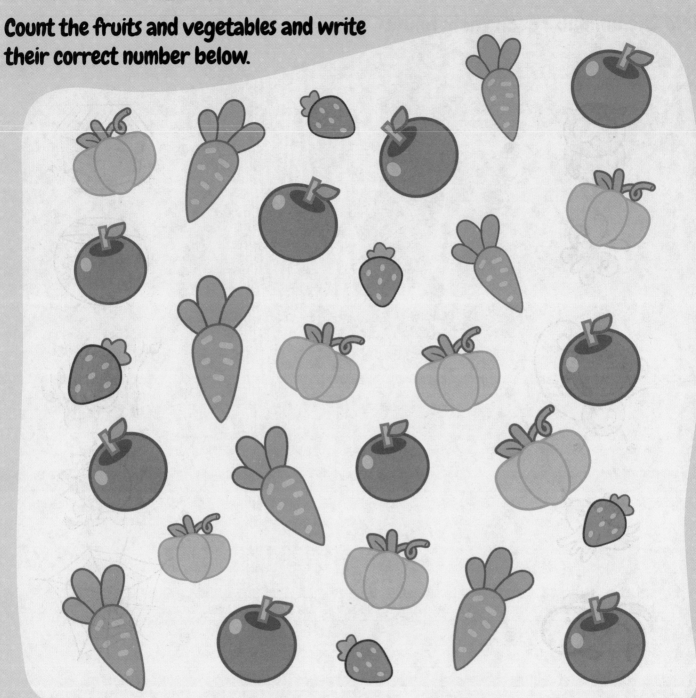

Bicycle Ride

Find the correct shadow of the boy.

Coral Reef

Spot 10 differences between the two pictures drawn below.

I Don't Fit Here

Find and circle the odd one out.

Garden Visitors

Solve the garden animals' crossword puzzle using picture clues.

Dino Trail

Help the dino reach its cub.

Deep Blue Ocean

Find 10 differences between the two pictures drawn below.

Fish Trail

Help the fish reach the shell by crossing the maze.

Expressive Shapes

Solve the shapes' word search puzzle by using the picture clues.

C	E	F	G	I	H	C	I	R	C	L	E
R	T	S	A	S	O	K	R	I	W	E	J
O	S	T	R	I	A	N	G	L	E	O	N
S	E	A	M	N	F	C	V	A	B	A	G
S	P	R	E	C	T	A	N	G	L	E	T
H	I	P	O	M	U	R	E	R	K	L	E
S	E	M	I	C	I	R	C	L	E	O	H
Q	P	I	D	M	A	O	T	C	R	A	E
U	S	K	U	I	M	W	V	S	R	E	A
A	Q	R	C	T	C	T	O	P	I	S	R
R	T	P	E	N	T	A	G	O	N	G	T
E	P	K	A	S	W	O	I	C	G	A	B

Circle   Cross   Star   Square   Heart

Triangle   Rectangle   Arrow   Pentagon   Ring

Semicircle

Answers

Jumbo Trail
Help the little elephant to find his mum.

Shadow Match
Match the animals of the cat family with their shadows.

Home Search
Help the creatures reach their home. The first one is done for you.

Pasture Fun
Can you spot 10 difference in the two pictures given below?

Pumpkin Patch
Find the exact mirror copy for each row and match the pairs . . .

ANSWERS:
1 – 2
3 – 6
4 – 5

Broom Flight
Find the correct shadow of the witch on the broom.

Picture Perfect
Find and circle two identical pictures.

Animal Pairs
Find and match identical animals. The first one is done for you.

Animal Crossword
Solve the animal crossword using the picture clues.

103

Answers

Pages 13-23

Cheese Trail
Help the hungry mouse reach the yummy cheese.

Happy Squirrels
Can you spot 5 differences between the two pictures below?

Freddy's Barn
Help Freddy count the animals in his barn.

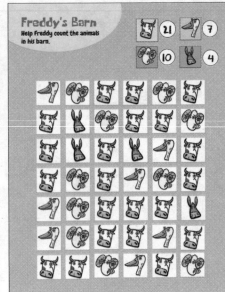

Shadow Match
Find the correct shadow of the woodpecker.

Sand Castle
Help the panda climb the correct set of ladders to reach his friends on the top.

Hopping Trail
Fill the missing numbers and help the frog reach the stone.

Evening Stroll
Spot 10 differences between the two pictures.

Zoo Animals
Complete the picture by identifying the missing patches. Draw the correct shape in the space given below.

Things That Move
Match vehicles with their mode of transportation.

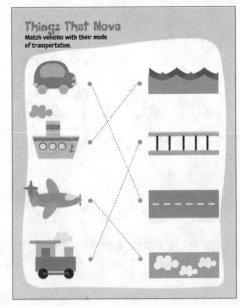

Answers Pages 24-32

Healthy Veggies
Solve the crossword with the help of picture clues.

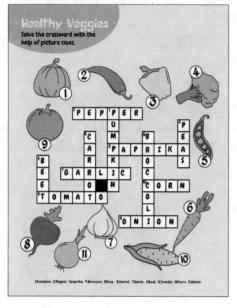

1.Pumpkin, 2.Pepper, 3.paprika, 4.Broccoli, 5.Peas, 6.Carrot, 7.Garlic, 8.Beat, 9.Tomato, 10.Corn, 11.Onion

Yummy Treat
Choose the yummy food which will complete the sequence.

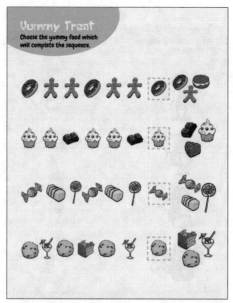

Turtle Twins
Find and match the turtle twins in the picture. The first one is done for you.

Entangled Giraffes
Free the entangled giraffes by connecting the numbers on the neck with the correct letters on the head.

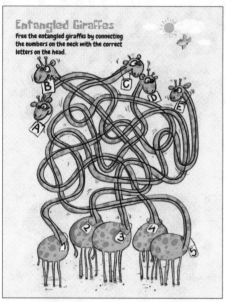

Exercising Panda
Match the pandas with their shadows.

Identical Twin
Find the identical image of the monkey on the left.

Grazing Cows
Find 10 differences between the two pictures below.

Honey Quest
Help the baby bear find his favorite food while avoiding the bees.

Expressive Dogs
Find and circle two identical pictures.

Answers

Answers **Pages 33-42**

Colorful Decorations
Count the objects and write the answers below.

Answers: 🪭 9 ▭ 5 🎀 10

Dancing Monkeys
Match the monkeys with their correct shadow.

Safari Fun
Spot 10 differences between the two pictures given below.

Jingle All The Way
Find two identical Santas in the picture and circle them.

Odd One Out
Find and circle the picture which does not belong to the group.

Shadow Fun
Find and circle the correct shadow of the children playing around the tree.

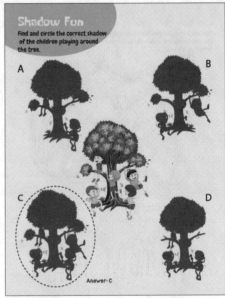

Answer: C

Zoo Visit
Use the picture clues to solve the crossword puzzle.

Jungle Animals
Match the animals with their shadows.

Pirate Ship
Find 10 differences between the two pictures drawn below.

106

Answers Pages 44-53

Animals in the Farm
Use the picture clues to solve the crossword puzzle.

1. Horse; 2. Sheep; 3. Turkey; 4. Pig; 5. Goat; 6. Rabbit; 7. Chick; 8. Duck; 9. Cow; 10. Chicken; 11. Donkey; 12. Dog; 13.Goose.

Farm Graze
Complete the picture by identifying the missing patches. Draw the correct shape in the space given below.

Space Travel
Spot 10 differences between the two pictures drawn below.

Animal Queue
Complete the sequence by choosing the correct animal.

Nut Quest
Help the squirrel grab the nut by finding the correct path.

Soccer Fun
Find the correct shadow of the soccer player.

Easter Egg
Help the painter find the right path to the giant Easter egg.

Mismatched Pictures
Can you match the faces of these cute animals with their bodies?

The Misfit
Find and circle the odd one out.

Answers

Animal Cruise
Find 10 difference between the two pictures drawn below.

Polar Trail
Help the baby polar bear find its mother.

Under The Ocean
Use the picture clues to solve the marine animals' word search puzzle.

F	S	Q	U	I	D	B	E	A	G	E	N
O	T	H	A	F	O	W	H	A	L	E	K
E	S	R	T	R	E	I	N	D	O	E	R
H	E	R	M	I	T	C	R	A	B	A	K
N	A	R	D	H	A	S	H	F	S	L	D
S	H	A	R	K	E	T	U	R	T	L	E
E	O	F	L	A	R	B	Z	A	E	P	B
O	R	I	R	M	A	N	T	A	R	A	Y
P	S	K	U	I	M	I	V	S	E	R	S
H	E	I	S	O	C	T	O	P	U	S	O
P	I	T	L	E	R	N	H	A	L	O	T
D	O	L	P	H	I	N	I	C	R	A	B

Squid	Whale	Lobster	Turtle	Shark
Sea Horse	Hermit Crab	Octopus	Manta Ray	Dolphin

Snail Trail
Help the snail find its way to its yummy food.

Spot The Odd One
Find and circle the odd one out in each row.

Hot Desert
Solve the desert animal crossword using the picture clues.

1. Centipede; 2. Cobra; 3. Armadillo; 4. meerkat; 5. Chameleon; 6. Rattlesnake; 7. Camel; 8. Vulture; 9. Scorpion.

African Safari
Solve the African animals' word search puzzle using the picture clues.

C	H	E	C	K	G	I	R	A	F	F	E
H	O	L	U	N	D	U	W	E	G	U	I
I	Z	E	B	R	A	E	I	C	O	Y	W
Q	P	P	T	H	C	K	U	D	U	I	I
O	J	H	F	I	Z	E	D	T	I	N	L
S	B	A	R	N	T	S	P	O	W	E	D
T	L	N	S	O	E	O	B	H	A	R	E
R	O	T	S	C	E	Y	Z	U	N	K	B
I	E	D	R	E	A	L	E	L	U	O	E
C	O	W	L	R	U	I	S	V	B	I	E
H	I	P	P	O	P	O	T	A	M	U	S
T	U	R	K	S	Y	N	A	T	H	I	T

Giraffe	Zebra	Wildebeest	Hare	Lion
Elephant	Ostrich	Hippopotamus	Rhinoceros	Kudu

Bat Terror
Spot 10 differences between the two pictures drawn below.

Skating Snowmen
Match each snowman with its correct shadow.

Answers

Jigsaw Puzzle

Identify the correct piece of the jigsaw puzzle to complete the picture of the lion.

Sportsmen

Help these players find their right sports equipment.

Missing Pieces

Help complete the picture by fitting the correct pieces of puzzle

A-5, B-4, C-3, D-1, E-2.

Polar Animals

Solve the polar animals' word puzzle using picture clues.

Polar Bear	Penguin	Killer Whale	Moose	Eagle
Walrus	Reindeer	Narwhal	Seal	Bison

Parking Area

Help the driver park the car in the parking area.

Missing Animals

Complete the picture by matching animals with their shapes.

Horse Pair

Find the exact mirror image of each horse and match the pairs.

Answer
1 - 4, 2 - 8, 3 - 6, 5 - 7.

Jungle Dance Party

Match the dancing animals with their shadows.

Cozy Homes

Help the animals reach their homes before nightfall.

109

Answers Pages 75-84

On The Farm
Solve this farm animals' word puzzle using the picture clues.

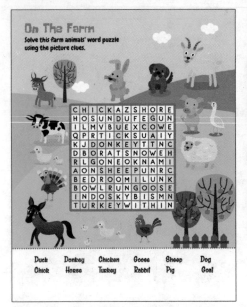

Duck	Donkey	Chicken	Goose	Sheep	Dog
Chick	Horse	Turkey	Rabbit	Pig	Goat

Bird Count
Count the birds and write the answers below.

Underground Trail
Help Buzzy cross the underground maze and reach its yummy food.

In The Swamp
Find 10 differences between the two pictures drawn below.

Jumping Reindeer
Match the reindeer with their correct shadows.

Elephant Jigsaw Puzzle
Identify the correct piece of the jigsaw puzzle to complete the picture.

Healthy Vegetables
Solve the vegetable word search puzzle using picture clues.

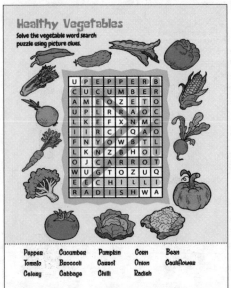

Pepper	Cucumber	Pumpkin	Corn	Bean
Tomato	Broccoli	Carrot	Onion	Cauliflower
Celery	Cabbage	Chilli	Radish	

Missing Frames
Find the fragments which will complete the picture.

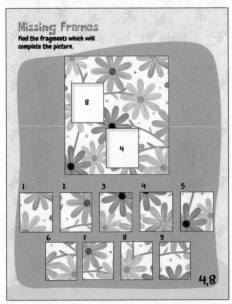

4,8

Night Stroll
Spot 10 differences between the two drawings.

Answers

Pages 85-94

Cloud Trail
Help the dinosaur reach its hungry babies.

Sports Mismatch
Can you find the 6 mistakes that the artist made while drawing the picture?

Pool Fun
Find the correct shadow of the boy.

Garden Fun
Count the animals and write the number in the space given below.

Out Of Place
Find and circle the odd one out.

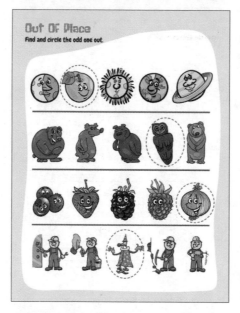

City Travel
Help the kids reach school on time.

Fruit Salad
Solve the fruit word search puzzle using the picture clues.

Coconut   Banana   Kiwi   Guava   Mango
Papaya   Mangosteen   Pomegranate   Orange   Apricot
Persimmon   Pineapple   Pear   Avocado

Animal Homes
Help the animals reach their houses.

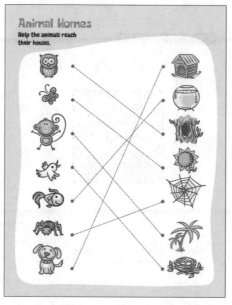

Farm Produce
Count the fruits and vegetables and write their correct number below.

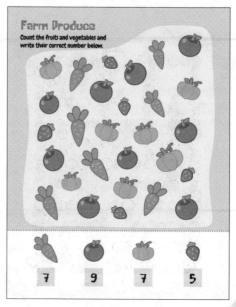

Answers

Bicycle Ride
Find the correct shadow of the boy.

Coral Reef
Spot 10 differences between the two pictures drawn below.

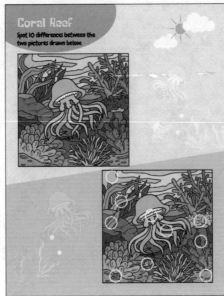

I Don't Fit Here
Find and circle the odd one out.

Garden Visitors
Solve the garden animals crossword puzzle using picture clues.

Dino Trail
Help the dino reach its cub.

Deep Blue Ocean
Find 10 differences between the two pictures drawn below.

Fish Trail
Help the fish reach the shell by crossing the maze.

Expressive Shapes
Solve the shapes' word puzzle by using the picture clues.

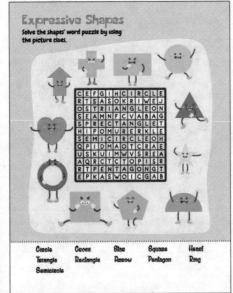